ERIB

Maria's Mysterious Mission

By Claudia Cangilla McAdam
Illustrated by Anna-Maria Crum
Photography by John Fielder

westcliffepublishers.com

Dedication

For my mother, Pat Cangilla, who made the words "mom" and "home" synonymous. –Claudia Cangilla McAdam

For Marci – my sister, my friend, my anchor. Love, Anna-Ree

International Standard Book Numbers
ISBN 10: 1-56579-588-1
ISBN 13: 978-1-56579-588-4

Editor: Kelly Smith
Designer: Anna-Maria L. Crum
Production Manager: Craig Keyzer

Published by:
Westcliffe Publishers, Inc.
3005 Center Green Dr.
Suite 220
Boulder, CO 80301

Printed in China

Library of Congress Cataloging-in-Publication Data:

McAdam, Claudia Cangilla.
Maria's mysterious mission / text by Claudia Cangilla McAdam ; illustrated by Anna-Maria L. Crum ; photography by John Fielder.
p. cm.
Summary: Maria, a homesick llama from South America, begins to love her new home in the Rocky Mountains after carrying a mysterious package for John the photographer.
ISBN-13: 978-1-56579-588-4
ISBN-10: 1-56579-588-1
[1. Llamas--Fiction. 2. Homesickness--Fiction. 3. Photography--Fiction. 4. Rocky Mountains--Fiction.] I. Crum, Anna-Maria, ill. II. Fielder, John, ill. III. Title.
PZ7.M47819Mar 2007
[E]--dc22

2007013733

For more information about other fine books and calendars from Westcliffe Publishers, please contact your local bookstore, call us at 1-800-258-5830, or visit us on the Web at **westcliffepublishers.com.**

Maria was homesick. She spent her days wandering in and out of the barn and poking around the corral. She hadn't cut a trail or carried a pack in months, not since she'd come to this new place in Colorado, far from her home in South America.

I don't belong here, she thought. Her eyes stung, and her throat felt tight. "I miss the Andes."

Maria didn't pay much attention when the rancher brought another man into the barn.

"I tell you, John, she's a hard worker," the rancher said. "That's why I brought her here."

"Can she carry all my gear?" John asked. "It's pretty heavy."

"Maria's your gal," the rancher answered.

Maria's ears pricked up. *¿Quién yo?* You mean me? Back in the Andes, whenever she had gotten a job, she would dance a little two-step on the tippy-tops of her two-toed feet. But not today. This wasn't home.

Riding in the trailer, Maria took no notice of the scenery that sped by. She missed the sharp, jagged mountains, the snowcapped peaks, the clear, cold lakes, and the lush highland meadows of the Andes.

¡Qué bonito! Maria thought. How pretty!

To take her mind off her homesickness, she tried to guess what kind of load she would be carrying. But she soon lost interest.

"Does it really matter?" she asked herself. "My work here couldn't be as important as what I did back home."

In South America, she had lugged heavy loads and sure-footed her way up muddy passes. She had trudged through deep snow. She'd been blinded by driving rain and baked by a blazing sun. And she had loved every minute of it.

John strapped the packs onto Maria. There was water and food. A small cook stove, a sleeping bag, and a tent. Then he plopped a mysterious pack on her back. And it was heavy!

As John led Maria, she thought about the timber she had carted through the Andes. The wood fed the fires that warmed Maria's people and cooked their food. Was there an ax in the pack on her back now? And a small saw? And ropes for bundling logs?

John took the mysterious pack from Maria and slung it on his back.

¡Si! Yes! Maria would discover what was in the bag and what their mission was. But John left her behind and walked too far away for her to see what he was doing. And when he came back, there was no wood strapped across his shoulders, no logs dragging behind him.

The following day took them farther into the mountains. As John hiked off with the pack, Maria helped herself to a crunchy snack of dried leaves. Nature's tortilla chips—*¡Que delicioso!* Yummy!

That reminded Maria of when she used to carry corn and potatoes to feed her people. Was John going to harvest crops? Perhaps the mysterious pack held a shovel, a sickle, and burlap bags for hauling food through the hills.

But when John returned, all he had was the pack. No burlap bags bulging with potatoes. No grain tumbling from sacks stuffed to the brim. Nothing.

The next day, Maria slogged through a downpour, the gear secure on her back.

"Are you wondering if it's worth it, Maria?" John asked.

She *was* wondering. In her old home, she had been like an ambulance carrying supplies to sick or injured people. Maybe John was a doctor. The pack could be filled with bandages and splints, a stethoscope and medicine. Yet they never stopped to help someone.

Maria pushed on, her eyelids flapping frantically—two windshield wipers gone wild. The muddy path sucked at her feet, and when the rain turned to ice crystals, snowflakes crusted her feathery eyelashes.

When the sun came out again, she was grateful for its heat. It reminded her of lugging sheared wool—including her own!—to the market to be woven into warm clothes and cuddly blankets for her people.

"Do you have clippers and scissors in that bag?" she wanted to ask John. Somehow she knew the answer was "no."

The next morning John came out of the tent with the pack. A man and a woman hiked up the path, leading their own llama. John set down the bundle and helped the couple check their map. Their llama wandered over to Maria.

"So what's in here?" The llama pawed at the bag.

"Move away, *señor.*" Maria pinned back her ears, stretched her long neck, and pointed her nose toward the sky. "Leave it alone, mister. I mean it!" She spit a warning shot into the air.

The llama ignored her and used his mouth to slide the zipper open a few inches. "Who needs thumbs when you have opposable lips?" he laughed.

That did it! Maria took aim and shot a long stream of green goop at him. Everything that a moment before had been in her stomach was now on his face. And it stunk!

John waved to the couple as they hurried their llama away. "Thanks for protecting my gear, Maria," he said. "Now, can you do something about your breath?"

At their next stop, John took the mysterious pack and opened it up.

¡Por fin! Finally! Maria was going to find out what was inside.

John assembled a tall, three-legged creature with a black box for a head. He could make its nose grow bigger, and he lifted up its black hair to look at something underneath.

Maria peered at the image on the back of the creature's head. It was the scene in front of her, only it was upside-down and backwards.

Maria gasped. She was in the Andes! At least, she could have been. Maria knew they were in the Rocky Mountains, but the scenery reminded her of home. Why hadn't she noticed that before?

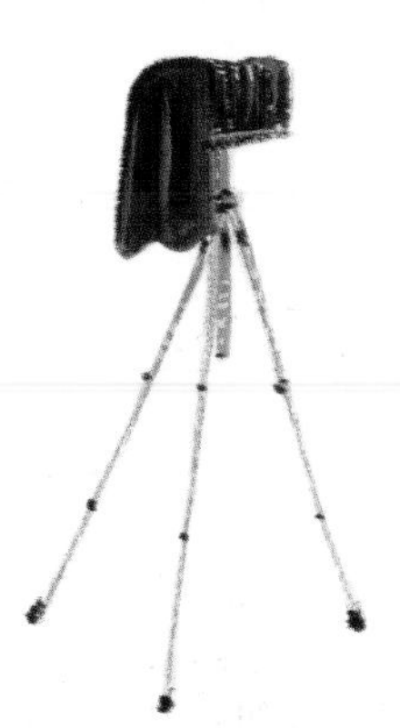

Maria carried John's camera and tripod for another three days while he took pictures.

They hiked down into deep rugged canyons.

They snaked up skinny paths and scaled high peaks that soared above the clouds.

“You’re the best llama I’ve ever worked with,” John told her as the sun set on their last day.

¡Gracias! Maria wanted to shout. Thank you!

The next time John visited the ranch, he brought a large package wrapped in brown paper.

"For Maria," he told the rancher.

John unwrapped the gift, and on the barn wall he hung a picture he had taken on their trip together. A picture of the Rocky Mountains that reminded Maria of the Andes.

Maria danced a little two-step on the tippy-tops of her two-toed feet. Her job *had* been important! She helped John bring the beauty of the mountains to everyone. More than that, Maria felt she was *home.*

Now Maria knew that her mysterious mission hadn't been the end of the good work she could do. In fact, it turned out to be just...

The beginning.